HOOLS

71541

Old MacDonald Had a Farm

Retold by Fay Robinson
Illustrations by Ann W. Iosa

SISKIYOU CO. SUPT. SCHOOLS
LIBRARY
609 S. GOLD ST.
YREKA, CA 96097

CHILDRENS PRESS®
CHICAGO

Library of Congress Cataloging-in-Publication Data

Robinson, Fay.
    Old MacDonald had a farm / by Fay Robinson : illustrated by
Ann W. Iosa.
        p.   cm.
    Summary: Bear goes to school with Nicki, learns the song "Old MacDonald
Had a Farm," and teaches it to the other stuffed animals at home.
    ISBN 0-516-02372-1
    [1. Toys—Fiction. 2. Animals—Fiction. 3. Singing—Fiction.]
I. Iosa, Ann W., ill. II. Title. III. Series: Robinson, Fay. Bear and alligator tales.
PZ7.R56564O1   1993
[E]—dc20   92-10757
                                                                CIP
                                                                 AC

Copyright © 1993 by Childrens Press®, Inc.
All rights reserved. Published simultaneously in Canada.
Printed in the United States of America.

1 2 3 4 5 6 7 8 9 10 R 02 01 00 99 98 97 96 95 94 93

One day, Bear went to school
with Nicki.

When Bear came home, he said
to Alligator, "I learned a wonderful
song in school. It's called
Old MacDonald Had a Farm. I'll
sing it for you."

4

"Wait!" said Alligator. "Who is Old MacDonald?"

"He's a farmer," said Bear.

"Wait!" said Alligator. "What does
E-I-E-I-O spell?"

"Nothing! It's what you sing
because there are no words there,"
said Bear.

And on his farm
he had a bear,
E-I-E-I-O.

With a grr, grr here and
a grr, grr there,
Here a grr, there a grr,
Everywhere a grr, grr.

"You sing this time, Alligator,"
said Bear.

"That's E-I-E-I-O, Alligator," said
Bear.

"I knew that," said Alligator.

With a snap, snap here and
a snap, snap there,
Here a snap, there a snap,
Everywhere a snap, snap.

With an oink, oink here and
an oink, oink there,
Here an oink, there an oink,
Everywhere an oink, oink.

With a snap, snap here and
a snap, snap there,
Here a snap, there a snap,
Everywhere a snap, snap.

28

29

"That was fun, Bear," said Alligator.
"But why did Old MacDonald have
a bear and an alligator on his farm?
Were they real animals? Or were they
stuffed animals, like us?"

"Oh, brother!" said Bear.

About the Author

Fay Robinson received a bachelor's degree in Child Study from Tufts University and a master's degree in Education from Northwestern University. She has taught preschool and elementary children and is the author of several picture books.

About the Artist

Ann W. Iosa received her professional training at Paier School of Art in New Haven, Connecticut. Her illustrations have appeared in numerous children's books, as well as in several popular magazines. Ann lives with her husband and two children in Southbury, Connecticut.